This book is given with love

TO:

_____

FROM:

_____

The Super Tiny Ghost

OCTOBER
27

Illustrated by:
Catty Flores

Written by:
Marilee Joy Mayfield

Once there was a super tiny ghost

He booed and screamed and moaned the most,

But no one noticed he was there

Not even children paused to stare.

He tried with all his tiny might
To scare them in their beds at night,
But they just thought he was a sheet
With big, black eyes and hidden feet.

He made a list of things to try

To make the humans scream and cry,

But everything he tried to do

Backfired and made him feel blue.

He watched the witches with their cats

And listened to the vampire bats.

He tried to learn their ghastly tricks

By watching monster horror flicks.

He wanted to be really spooky

But he came off strange and oddly kooky.

Being a ghost just isn't any fun

If you can't make people scream and run.

He even went to scary school

To study being mean and cruel,

But when he tried to terrify

They paid no mind, which made him cry.

It would soon be time for Halloween
And in his heart he had a dream,
He wanted to be wild and frightening
With boos like thunder and eyes like lightning.

So he floated softly through the door

Of the local party costume store.

Everyone would scream and race away

When this new scary ghost came out to play!

They had scary monsters and hairy beasts

Vampires, zombies, and voodoo priests

Creepy spiders and spell-casting witches

And mummies all wrapped up in stitches.

TRICK OR TREAT

Dressing Room

He picked the best costume off the last rack
And stuck it inside a trick-or-treat sack.
When he tried it on in the dressing room
He was the perfect picture of doom and gloom.

He had blood on his forehead and a toothless grin
Warts on his neck and bright green skin,
He walked like a mummy with a lurching pace
Only a mother could love that face!

When he went back out into the store

People screamed and ran for the door.

Now he was ready to frighten and scare

No one would laugh now--they wouldn't dare!

A few days passed, it was Halloween night

The streets were lit by jack o'lantern light,

And the humans in costumes, both young and old

Wandered into the dark, crisp, autumn cold.

The tiny ghost had the best disguise

But much to his horror and great surprise

No one he met screamed or ran away

They just thought he was there to play.

Except for one tiny baby--her eyes went wide,
She let out a piercing scream...and then she cried.
And suddenly the super tiny ghost felt so sad
Making this baby scream made him feel bad.

So he stopped for a moment and took off his head
And popped out with his tiny ghost-head instead.
Then the baby started laughing and he felt complete
She patted his round head and gave him a treat.

♥ Claim Your FREE Gift!

Visit ➡ PDICBooks.com/tinyghost

Thank you for purchasing The Super Tiny Ghost,
and welcome to the Puppy Dogs & Ice Cream family.

We're certain you're going to love the little gift we've
prepared for you at the website above.

Made in the USA
Middletown, DE
01 October 2020

20846949R00024